The
Pirate's Revenge

ReadZone Books Limited

www.ReadZoneBooks.com

© in this edition 2017 ReadZone Books Limited

This print edition published in cooperation with Fiction Express, who first published this title in weekly instalments as an interactive e-book.

FICTION EXPRESS

Fiction Express
Boolino Limited
First Floor Office, 2 College Street,
Ludlow, Shropshire SY8 1AN
www.fictionexpress.co.uk

Find out more about Fiction Express on pages 81–82.

Design: Laura Harrison & Keith Williams
Cover Image: Bigstock

© in the text 2016 Stewart Ross
The moral right of the author has been asserted.

ISBN 978-1-78322-604-7

Printed in Malta by Melita Press

The Pirate's Revenge

Stewart Ross

FICTION EXPRESS

What do other readers think?

Here are some comments left on the Fiction Express blog about this book:

"I love your book."
Oscar, Derbyshire

"I love all of the chapters. I have read them over and over again. Thanks so much Stewart for making this great book."
Nathan, Somerset

"Hi. I adore your book! How do you write so good? It's amazing!"
Jasmine, Stockport

"I have read your book The Pirate's Revenge. *It is really good and I can't wait to read another book."*
James, Surrey

"I like The Pirate's Revenge. *I like the mystery. I like how it would have been like in that time."*
Lucas, Manchester

Contents

Chapter 1

The Warning!

Why, I wondered, do seafaring folk always sing of disasters? Old Jacob Winstanley, who had weathered more storms than anyone I know, was in full cry. He stood before the fire of our inn, the Friendly Frenchman, and bellowed out the last verse of his song of shipwreck:

*"Then three times 'round went
our gallant ship,*

And three times 'round went she,

And the third time that she went 'round

She sank to the bottom of the sea!"

Despite the cosy atmosphere in the bar, I shivered. I had been to sea. I had seen waves as tall as our church spire; I had felt the ship's timbers beneath me groan as if in pain; I had been slapped by gales strong enough to tear the sails from the spars.

No, I never wished to go to sea again.

The roaring of the chorus interrupted my thoughts:

"Oh the ocean waves may roll,

And the stormy winds may blow,

While we poor sailors go skipping aloft

And the land lubbers lay down below,
below, below

And the land lubbers lay down below."

The shanty ended with a great roar of
approval. A dozen rosy-cheeked faces
turned towards my father and myself.

"Hey! John Tregorey, call yourself a
landlord?" bellowed Old Jacob. "More
ale for my shipmates!" He turned his
bleary eyes in my direction. "And you,
young Arden Tregorey, shake a leg! Look
sharp and fetch me a beaker of rum!"

I moved towards the bar. As I did
so, out of the corner of my eye I saw
the inn door open. A figure stepped
inside and closed the door behind
him. For a moment I didn't think
much of it. The Friendly Frenchman

was well-liked and its front door was never still for long.

But there was something about this new arrival that made me look again. I stared in disbelief. No, I thought, it's impossible. He's dead.

Except he wasn't. There, as tall, lean and mean-eyed as when I had last seen him on the island of Hispaniola, stood Ebenezer Dag.

I hurried behind the bar and reached for the loaded pistol we always kept there. As I did so, a sharp, cruel voice froze the atmosphere in the bar like a north wind.

"No need for that, young Arden," said Dag, twisting his mouth into a contorted smile. "Ebenezer's no pirate no longer. Reformed man, he be."

At a nod from my father, I put the pistol down. But whether Dag was reformed or not, his arrival put an end to the fun for the evening. He was well-known in every port in the land, and not even Old Jacob wished to spend time with him.

Five minutes later, father and I found ourselves alone with a man we had thought dead, murdered by his own captain.

"Now we can talk," he began after the final customer had shuffled off into the storm raging outside. "But have no fears. As I told ye, I be a reformed man. God-fearing now, I be."

"So why're ye here?" asked father, his face lined with anxiety.

"I be 'ere," said Dag slowly, looking at each of us in turn, "with a warning!"

The moment Old Jacob had started singing that shipwreck shanty, I knew something bad was going to happen. And here it was.

Dag reported that my old enemy, the dastardly pirate Lambert Spain, had escaped from prison on the island of Hispaniola. Nicknamed 'Luggole' after he lost one of his ears in a fight, Spain was feared throughout the Caribbean – and beyond – as one of the cruellest and cleverest of all sea bandits.

A year ago, after a long and terrifying adventure, I had captured him single handed as he was trying to get away with a brass-bound chest containing the priceless McKinley jewels. I had brought the villain back to land, but the jewels had sunk to the bottom of the sea.

"And that," Dag explained, drinking deep from the glass of rum my father had provided, "is why I's 'ere, young Arden. Luggole 'as sworn revenge, bloody revenge! I 'eard 'im in a tavern in Port Royal, Jamaica. He's goin' to scour the sea-bed, raise that treasure chest and use the money to buy a vessel."

His face was now no more than six inches from mine. "He'll do a bit of piratin', of course, but not 'afore he's come 'ere after ye! 'Skin that Arden Tregorey alive,' that's what he said he'd do. I 'eard it wi' me own ears – and I got two," he added with a dreadful chuckle.

So that was it. Luggole Spain wanted revenge. And Ebenezer Dag, once a member of Spain's crew, had come here to warn me. I thanked him warmly and asked what he advised me to do.

He closed his eyes and, as if thinking out loud, said there was no point in running away because Luggole would hunt me down wherever I went. No, the answer was to get to the jewels before he did. Spain and I were the only people who knew where they lay. If I could recover them before he got his hands on them, he'd have no means of resuming his vile career. And no means of coming after me, either.

Dag didn't have much more to say. After asking me – no, begging me – to "do what's right", he shook my hand and limped out of the door into the blackness of the night.

Chapter 2

Shipwrecked!

I didn't sleep a wink that night.
Father told me to forget the whole
thing. It was just a drunken story, he
said. Ebenezer Dag had always been
a lying rogue and always would be.

But, young and foolish as I was, I
couldn't get Dag's words out of my head.
"Do what's right," he had said. I
thought of nothing but Luggole's threat
to skin me alive and of the hundreds of
poor sailors who would suffer if he got
a ship and resumed his terrible trade.

I had money and I could leave my studies for a few weeks, I told myself. I could make a quick passage to Hispaniola, hire a diver to recover the treasure.... Ah! If only I had listened to my poor father's wise words and thought through my crazy plan more carefully!

As it was, the following morning I packed a few clothes and other possessions into a canvas bag, bade heartfelt farewells to my friends and to my weeping father, and set out for the great port of Bristol. Though I had sworn never to go to sea again, I felt a tingle of excitement at being in the harbour again: the cry of gulls, the forest of tall masts, and the sharp, sweet smell of tar.

I had no trouble finding a vessel sailing to the Caribbean and that very afternoon boarded the *Neptune*, bound for Trinidad. From there it would be easy to cross to Hispaniola.

Just one incident gave me small cause for concern. Watching the crew coming aboard the *Neptune*, I noticed two of them chatting to a third man in the shadows at the far end of the quay. They were more than 100 yards away, so I could easily have been mistaken, but the tall fellow they were talking to looked familiar.

Almost like Ebenezer Dag.

I suppose there was no reason why an old sea dog like him shouldn't be on down here on the quayside. But, somehow, he just looked suspicious.

* * *

I soon forgot the incident and set about making myself comfortable for the voyage. Comfortable? Captain Gilbertson said he had never seen seas like it. Day after day the wind screamed in the rigging like a pack of wounded animals, while the great green waves crashed mercilessly over the decks. I was terrified, and couldn't get the words of Old Jacob's song out of my head: 'sank to the bottom of the sea!'

Oh! How I wished I had listened to my dear father and stayed at home!

The closer we drew to Trinidad, the worse the weather grew. The climax came just as dawn was breaking on the forty-second day of our voyage. Peering through the spray ahead, I made out the dim grey shape of a rocky shoreline.

Moments later, the *Neptune* shuddered violently. With a dreadful crack, the foremast split and fell into the sea.

The sailors around me exchanged terrified glances. What was it? I asked. What was that dreadful noise?

Tom Drake, a young mariner I had become friendly with, shouted above the noise of gale, "We're aground, Arden! Struck a reef! Save yourself, my friend! Save yourself!"

Before I could reply, I felt a steely grip on my shoulder. It was Cadan, one of the two sailors I'd seen talking suspiciously on the quayside in Bristol.

"That's right, Arden," he growled. "We's aground and sinkin' fast. But put yer trust in me and mi mate, Jago. We'll see ye come to no harm!"

Chapter 3

A Helping Hand

When I gave no reply, Cadan's fierce grip tightened on my shoulder. "I told ye, Tregorey," he shouted above the howling of the storm, "me and my mate Jago'll see ye come to no harm."

No harm? The man's harsh tone and cruel grasp were no marks of friendship, and I didn't believe him. My mind flashed back to the quayside in Bristol. What *had* he and Jago been talking to Dag about?

Whatever it was, I was sure they were up to no good. I was in double danger, from the *Neptune* breaking up around me, and now from these rogues.

"Thankee," I yelled as I struggled to free myself. "But I'll take my chance in the lifeboat."

"That's what ye think," growled Cadan. He began dragging me across the lurching deck away from the rest of the crew.

"Help!" I screamed. "Someone help me! Please!"

At that moment, the vessel gave a violent heave, Cadan lost his balance and I wriggled free. Fighting my way against the gale, I struggled across the slippery deck towards where the lifeboat had been. Too late. It was already in the water and moving rapidly away.

I looked round to see Caden and Jago advancing towards me. There was only one way out. Without thinking what I was doing, I vaulted over the side of the ship and into the raging sea.

My memory of what happened next is blurred. I can remember the taste of salt in my mouth, my nose and my lungs as I was tossed like a twig on the heaving waves. I am a strong swimmer, but the shore was a hundred paces distant.

With each stroke my arms grew weaker. I felt myself getting sucked down. Once again, the words of the sea shanty came echoing back to haunt me:... *and she sank to the bottom of the sea!*

I think I must have passed out. The next thing I remember was lying on a sandy beach with a broad black face looking down at me. *Have I died?* I thought.

Then the face spoke to me. "You're safe now, young lad. No worrying!"

"Thank – you!" I spluttered. Then I passed out once more.

* * *

When I came to, the storm was dying down and clear patches of brilliant blue dotted the sky above me. My rescuer explained that his name was Oloudah. He had been near the shore and had seen our shipwreck. Some of the crew had got away in a lifeboat, and he was just about to leave when he spotted me, half drowned, battling through the surf towards the beach.

I couldn't leave you to drown," he said, with a friendly smile. "So I swam out and pulled you in. Like a Good Samaritan, eh?"

I thanked him again and eagerly ate some of the bananas he brought from a nearby grove. When the sun finally appeared and began to dry my drenched clothes, I explained to him who I was and why I was there.

"And you?" I asked when I had finished. "What were you doing on the beach in the middle of a storm?"

He did not reply and turned away from me. As he did so, I noticed the initials SC branded onto his bare shoulder. Then I understood: Oloudah was a runaway slave. The knowledge made me like him even more – this hunted man with a price on his head had risked his life to save a total stranger.

Father and I hated the very idea of slavery, and my meeting with Oloudah gave me a chance to strike a small blow for freedom. I wanted to get to Hispaniola and raise the jewel chest from the sea bed before Luggole Spain got his hands on it. If Oloudah came with me, he'd be a free man: Jamaica was English and Hispaniola was French – no French colony would return a slave to an English one.

From that moment onwards, Oloudah and I were a team.

To reach Hispaniola, we needed a boat. Oloudah was unwilling to steal one. If he were caught, he said, the punishment for theft as well as running away would surely be death.

There was no need to steal, I explained with a grin. My gold sovereigns were still safe inside the pouch strapped beneath my shirt. While my new friend remained in hiding, I'd walk along the shore to the nearest settlement, hire a small boat and sail her back here. We would then set out together for Hispaniola.

Oloudah had been to Port Antonio on errands for his master, Samuel Collins, and he reckoned it was no more than a couple of hours' walk away. On the outskirts of the village, I'd find a small jetty manned by an old fisherman named Joseph. He'd be happy to hire out his boat for a moderate fee.

Chapter 4

To Hispaniola

The plan worked out almost perfectly. I say 'almost' because when I asked Joseph whether I could hire his boat, he gave me a quizzical look.

"Hire my boat?" he repeated. "Odd. That's the second offer I've had today."

When I inquired what he meant, he said that two strangers had come by with the same request. On being told the price – sixpence a day, with six guineas in advance – they had cursed him, called him a swindling old dog and threatened him with violence.

But Joseph had stood his ground and they had gone away to look elsewhere.

"You don't happen to remember their names, do you?" I asked, feeling fairly sure I knew the answer.

"Unusual," said Joseph, scratching his sunburned cheek. "I know the one called himself Jago and t'other was something like 'Cajun'."

I thanked him and handed over the money for the boat. As I sailed out of the bay and headed back towards Oloudah, I thought about what I had learned. First, Jago and Cadan had survived the shipwreck. Second, they wanted a boat, which meant they too were probably headed for Hispaniola.

They wouldn't know I was still alive – unless they returned and spoke to Joseph. In which case, Oloudah and I had to be very, very careful.

* * *

Joseph's boat had been fitted out for long fishing trips. A canvas awning sheltered us from the sun, and there was a small iron water tank and plenty of lockers for storage. Having loaded her with nuts and fruit, and water from a nearby stream, we set sail. I had a pretty clear idea of the geography of the Caribbean from my previous adventures, and I knew how to navigate by the sun and stars. If we went east from Jamaica, we were bound to hit Hispaniola sooner or later.

Joseph's boat was well made but heavy, and I was grateful for Oloudah's help with the sails and tiller. Nevertheless, with the trade winds steady on our starboard side, we made good speed, and on the evening of the third day, the grey hills of Hispaniola loomed on the horizon.

"Freedom!" sighed Oloudah. "Thank you, young Arden. Without you, I don't know how–"

His words were interrupted by a loud 'BOOM!' Moments later, something splashed into the sea alongside us. We had been so wrapped up in the sight ahead we had failed to notice a large schooner creeping up behind us. A second shot from its cannon quickly brought us to our senses.

The vessel was quicker than ours, and soon she was only a few feet behind us. Against the darkening sky we noticed a man leaning over the prow and grinning. As he lifted a lantern to his face, an evil leer chilled the tropical air. It was Jago.

"Ahoy there, shipmates!" he cried. "Bargain time!"

"Never!" I cried.

"I'm not a-talkin' a-ye," he sneered. "I'm addressin' the runaway slave they's searchin' all Jamaica for. Listen, Oloudah. Hand over that brat Arden Tregorey and we'll let ye go on to Hispaniola. If ye don't, ye'll be taken back in chains to yer master for him to do with ye as he pleases. Ha-ha-ha! Now, answer me slave! Answer!"

Chapter 5

The Fight

I looked across at Oloudah. "Reckon we could make a run for it?" I asked. "It's already quite dark–"

"No lad," he interrupted, shaking his head and sucking in air through his teeth. "There's no escape – and I'm not handing you over to those vermin."

"But… but they'll take you back to Jamaica!"

Our conversation was interrupted by a roar from the schooner astern of us. "Made up yer mind, slave?" bellowed

Jago. "Give ye count of ten, then we's a-comin' in! One…"

My heart thumped against my ribs and, despite the cool of the evening breeze, sweat broke out on the palms of my hands. "Do as they ask, Oloudah," I pleaded. "Hand me over and you can go free. They can't afford to harm me, and I'm sure I'll be able to get away."

"Four…"

Oloudah grunted. "Don't be a fool, Arden. Think they can be trusted? There's but one way out, and that's to fight. Listen, I've got a plan…."

"Seven… eight…"

After he had given me a hurried outline of his idea, Oloudah shouted back to Jago, "Very well, sir. Have the boy. But you won't take me!" With that, he sprang onto the side rail and dived into the sea.

Jago let out a peal of cruel laughter. "Goodbye slave! Think I cared about ye? Pah! It's the boy as I wants. And to make sure he don't go gettin' away...."

A match flared next to the cannon in the schooner's bows. A moment later, there was a flash of flame, a tremendous CRACK! and the sound of smashing timbers. The shot had been cunningly aimed at the waterline below where I was standing. I could already hear the sea rushing in through the hole.

The boat I was on was sinking – and there was nothing I could do about it.

As the schooner moved alongside my stricken vessel, I saw the familiar faces of Jago and Cadan on the forecastle.

A third man stood beside them and I could just make out a fourth at the wheel on the quarterdeck. More members of the gang or just hired crew? I soon found out.

Oloudah had told me to play for time. With three of my enemies gathered around the lantern in the schooner's bow, I saw my opportunity. I vaulted onto their ship and grabbed the ratlines that ran up the main mast. Quick as a cat, I began to climb.

Jago, Cadan and their companion ambled back and stood looking up at me. "No 'scape up there, boy," yelled Cadan. "Kitto, shin up aloft and bring the scurvy knave down! We want him alive, remember."

I felt the ropes shudder as the rogue began his ascent. Scurrying the last few feet to the narrow crow's nest, I looked anxiously towards the stern. Oloudah should be there by now, surely? I glanced down. Kitto was already halfway up the lines and would be upon me in a matter of seconds.

What happened next is little more than a blur in my memory. Oloudah had swum a few strokes away from the schooner underwater, then doubled back unseen and sneaked on board through an open gun port. Emerging below the quarterdeck, he crept up behind Jago and Cadan and knocked them out cold with a mallet he'd brought from below deck.

Meanwhile, Kitto had scrambled up the last ten feet of the ratlines and grabbed at my ankles. I clung on to the mast and I kicked down as hard as I could with both feet. The blow caught my assailant full on the chest. He lost his grip and, with a muffled cry, arced backwards into the inky ocean below.

The fourth member of the gang abandoned the wheel the moment he saw the attack on his colleagues. Snatching up his cutlass, he uttered a fearful oath and charged across the deck towards Oloudah. It was no contest. My friend waited until the villain was almost on him. He then sidestepped neatly, grabbed him by the waist and hurled him headlong into the sea beside Kitto.

We had no time to congratulate ourselves on our victory or to watch as poor Joseph's boat disappeared beneath the waves. With no one at the helm the schooner was lurching wildly; above our heads the sails flapped like the wings of a giant bird. We also couldn't ignore the pitiful cries from the two men in the sea. So while Oloudah fished them out and tied them up with Jago and Cadan, I took the wheel and brought the vessel back on course for Hispaniola.

By now night had fallen and the sea glimmered beneath a thin sliver of moon and a million brilliant stars. Bright though it was – far brighter than any night sky back in England – we decided not to attempt to enter a port on an unknown coastline at night. We lowered the sails, stretched ourselves out upon them and waited for sunrise.

Chapter 6

Luggole Spain

Shortly after dawn we dropped anchor off a small village that I later learned was called Jérémie. It would be safer to go ashore here, I decided, rather than in the capital, Port-au-Prince.

How wrong I was!

When I asked Oloudah what he was going to do now he was a free man, he smiled and said he'd stay with me until I had recovered the jewels.

"Then you're the best man on Earth," I gasped, shaking him warmly by the hand. "And I don't know how to thank'ee enough."

He simply shrugged and said he was only doing what any honest person would do for a friend. It wasn't true, of course, but there was no point in arguing.

After breakfasting on food from the schooner's galley, I left Oloudah on board to guard the prisoners and went into the town for fresh supplies. I was also keen to find out from the locals whether they had any news of my old enemy.

The first person I spoke to, a young woman selling dried tobacco leaves in the market, gave me an uneasy feeling. At the mention of the name 'Lambert Spain' she looked away, pretending not to have heard me.

"You – him – must – be knowing!"'
I said in my broken French. "Infâme –
an infamous pirate!"

She gave me a terrified glance,
gathered up her leaves and walked
away. Well, I thought, that's a fine
start! Why on earth is she so frightened
of a name?

I was sure the man himself was in
Port-au-Prince. After all, that's where
the jewels were – almost. They were
actually in 20 feet of water just off the
shore – precisely where, only I knew.

That's why Luggole had sent Dag,
Jago and Cadan to capture me. Now
they had failed, I reasoned that the
pirate's only chance was to try to ambush
me in Port-au-Prince when I turned up
there to recover the treasure.

I couldn't have known it, but he wasn't in Port-au-Prince. He understood the authorities would be watching for him after his jailbreak and, too clever to do the obvious thing, he had chosen to lie low in a little fishing village. Its name was Jérémie.

* * *

We ran into each other around noon, shortly after I had finished buying our supplies. I was asking the quickest way back to the quay; he was coming out of a grubby-looking rum shop. There he was, just as I remembered him: medium height, dressed in a frayed coat of scarlet wool, hatless, and with his black hair tied back in a tarry pigtail.

But it wasn't the coat that gave him away, nor the pigtail. It was the livid scar and dark hole where his left ear had been.

His eyes narrowed when he saw me. "So 'ere ye are, Tregorey," he sneered. "Well, ain't I a lucky man?"

As he turned back towards the rum shop to summon the rest of his gang, I did the only thing I could. I ran.

I ran down the dusty street and across the cobbled quay to where I had moored the skiff in which I had come ashore. The small rowing boat was still there, just as I had left her. I scrambled aboard, put the oars in the rowlocks and glanced over my shoulder to make sure I was heading in the direction of the schooner.

The schooner? I had left her riding at anchor no more than 50 yards from the shore. And now... I glanced left and right. She was nowhere to be seen.

Chapter 7

Vanished!

I stopped rowing and turned to take a better look ahead. No, there was no sign of the schooner. The ship, with our four prisoners and my friend Oloudah on board, had vanished.

I shifted back to face the stern and picked up the oars. As I did so, I saw Luggole Spain and half-a-dozen scrawny-looking men hurrying onto the quayside.

"Don't be so hasty, young Arden," the pirate shouted. "Come back 'ere an' you an' me can do some business. Treasure business."

I didn't even waste my breath replying. I'd rather have done a deal with the Devil himself than with that villain. But what had happened to our ship? Having rowed further from the shore in case the pirates took a shot at me, I tried to figure it out.

I decided the schooner must have slipped her anchor in the stiff breeze and drifted round the headland out of sight. Oloudah wouldn't have been able to sail the two-masted vessel on his own, so it was up to me to find her.

It was not such a good idea. By the time I reached the open sea, there was still no sign of the vessel I was seeking, and the stiff breeze had blown up into a squall. My little rowing boat bounced around like a puppy, and it took all my strength to keep her pointing into to the waves. If I had let her go sideways on, the sea would have rolled her over in an instant.

There was no hope of steering a course, either – I just had to go where the wind took me. I laboured for the rest of the day until, as night closed in, the wind fell and the sea grew calmer.

Exhausted, I lay down on the bottom of my boat and fell into a deep sleep.

* * *

I awoke at sunrise and took stock of my position. I was not more than a mile from the shore and, carried along by a swift current, was moving due east at some speed. As I ate some of the bread and fruit I'd bought ashore, I pictured the chart of Hispaniola in my mind. If I was travelling east, sooner or later I'd reach Port-au-Prince. And there, on a reef just off shore, lay the treasure.

But first I had to find the missing schooner with my friend Oloudah on board. They must have been driven along by the same wind and current as me, I reasoned. In which case, they couldn't be too far away.

I was right. Shortly after noon, when the sun was at its highest, the buildings and jetties of Port-au-Prince came into sight. And there, anchored in the bay, was the schooner!

Pulling hard on the oars, I quickly came to within twenty yards of the vessel's stern. I had stopped rowing and was about to shout up at Oloudah, when a figure came on deck. A familiar figure, but not the one I had been expecting. It was Jago!

I spun the boat round and headed for the shore, hoping I had not been spotted. What on earth was going on? Oloudah would never have released the prisoners. That left only one possibility: somehow they must have escaped and taken control of the vessel. If that was the case, what had they done with the kind, honourable man who had saved my life?

I must admit, at that moment a small, frightened part of me wanted to fish out the jewels and return home as quickly as I could. But I couldn't abandon

Oloudah. Besides, it'd be impossible to dive for the treasure without Luggole and his dastardly crew noticing. The moment they saw what was going on, they'd be on to me like bees round a honey pot.

I needed information. I pulled my skiff onto a muddy bank to the west of the port and made my way into the town. It was just as shabby as I remembered it. The streets were filthy, faded paint peeled off the wooden houses, and the citizens I met had downcast, haunted expressions. It was as if fear of piracy had entered their very bones.

I made my way to the church in the hope of finding Father Benedicto, the priest who had helped me once before.

No, I was told in a strange mixture of Spanish and French by a woman sweeping the steps, Padre Benedicto had gone to another island.

"*Promoción!*" she grinned, resuming her sweeping.

Well, he deserved a promotion, I thought. But it would have been nice to find someone friendly to talk to. As it was, I had to make do with a young man selling tots of rum from a stall near the harbour.

"That ship out there," I asked, pointing at the schooner, "who does it belong to?"

The man shrugged. "No know."

I had a silver coin ready in my hand and gave it to him. "Tell me, *por favor.*"

He examined the coin, bit it and

glanced around nervously. "Ship come this morning," he whispered. "They say no good men on board. Have prisoner."

Prisoner? My heart jumped. It must be Oloudah! So he was still alive. "Tell me more!" I pleaded.

But the man either knew nothing or was too terrified to speak further. I thanked him and set off towards where I'd hidden the skiff. If the pirate crew had sailed here once they'd taken control of the schooner, I reasoned, then Luggole was almost certainly expected here, too.

I had to be very careful.

Chapter 8

Prisoners

Once in the shade of the trees surrounding the town, I settled down to wait for nightfall. I must have dozed off, for when I awoke it was quite dark. Finding my way by starlight, I walked carefully to my boat, put one foot on board – and froze.

"Glad ye's rowin' out to yon schooner, Arden m'dear," said a harsh and familiar voice, "'cos me and my mate Cadan is wantin' a passage there too."

As he spoke, Luggole clamped a hand on my shoulder. There was no escape.

He or one of his gang must have seen me come ashore. They'd then spoken to the rum seller, guessed at my plan and waited here to ambush me.

With reluctant strokes I rowed the three of us to the schooner where we were hauled aboard. There, standing in a grim reception committee, stood Jago, Kitto and the fourth man, whom I soon learned was called Ruan.

"Another captive for the prison ship!" chortled Luggole, kicking me painfully on the shins. "An' this one'll be even more use than t'other, eh mates?"

"So long as 'ee can swim," smirked Jago. At this, the others roared with vulgar laughter.

"Take 'im below, Ruan, and chain 'im up with the slave," commanded Luggole.

"I'll be takin' a tot o' rum afore explainin' to 'im what we's a-wantin'."

The only ray of light on that terrible evening was seeing Oloudah again and finding that he had suffered nothing more than a little bruising. His story was as I had guessed – after Kitto had cut through his ropes with a piece of broken bottle, the prisoners had overpowered Oloudah and seized control of the schooner.

No sooner had my friend finished his story than Luggole appeared. His face was flushed. He'd take Oloudah back to Jamaica and collect a reward for his recapture, he explained. But my prospects were much better, he added. The expression on his scarred face was half-sneer, half-leer.

"All ye gotta do, Arden, is show us where that treasure be and 'elp us haul it out – and I'll give ye half and let ye go free. Kind, ain't I?"

I said nothing.

His eyes narrowed. "Of course, if ye refuses, I might be a little less… generous, mightn't I?"

"You know my answer," I said, trying to sound braver than I actually felt. "I'll never, never do anything for you except hand you over to the authorities to be locked away. This time, I hope, for life!"

He gave a heavy, false sigh. "Very well, Master Arden. It's no food or water for ye until ye chooses to 'elp us. Good night!"

He stomped back up the stairs, and before long the deck above echoed to sound of singing and clashing tankards.

As the night wore on, the pirates' voices grew louder and more slurred. But not so slurred that I couldn't understand something I heard Luggole say.

"An' when we've raised that there chest with them jewels in it," he roared, "We'll cast it back into the sea. An' this time it won't have treasure in it – it'll have Arden Tregorey! Ha-ha-ha!"

"Does we 'have to drown 'im?" I heard Ruan ask. "Af'er all, 'ee's only a lad. And that slave fella, 'ee did as pull Jago an' me from the sea. 'Ee din't 'ave to…"

He was cut short by the sound of a tankard thumping into the deck.

"Enough of that preacher's talk, shipmate," growled Luggole. "Either Tregorey goes down or ye do, got it?"

"Aye, aye, Cap'n Spain," came the sullen reply.

An hour or so later, the noise of carousing had been replaced by snores. I lay awake for hours listening to the gentle lapping of the sea and thinking over what Luggole had said. Then, as I was finally dropping off to sleep, I heard a creak on the stairs. I sat up sharply and saw a shadowy figure silently approaching out of the darkness.

Chapter 9

An Old Friend

A shaft of moonlight lay between the stairway and the corner where Oloudah and I were chained. As the mysterious figure advanced, the pale light fell briefly on a familiar face.

For a second I thought I was dreaming. Impossible! What on earth was Tom Drake, my friend from the *Neptune*, doing here on this schooner? Surely he hadn't joined the pirate gang?

Of course he hadn't. Kneeling at my side, he explained that he was here to help.

I thanked him as warmly as I could without raising my voice. From the dampness of his clothing, I guessed he must have swum out to the ship. "But how did you know where I was?" I whispered.

He'd tell me his story later, he said. All that mattered now was getting Oloudah and me out of the hands of the five villains asleep on deck. I woke Oloudah and explained who Tom was and how he was risking his life to rescue us.

Oloudah said he was hugely grateful – but wasn't sure what Tom could do. We examined the padlocked shackles that held us, looking for a fault, a weakness. Nothing. Without a blacksmith's tools, we could be released only by unlocking the padlock. And to do that we'd need the key I had seen Luggole Spain place deep in the pocket of his scarlet coat.

"Tis no matter, Arden," whispered Tom. "We're near the shore. I swam out to this ship, so I can swim back again. Now I know for sure what's going on, I'll get the constables out here and they'll set ye free in no time."

But no sooner were the words out of his mouth, than we heard someone stirring on the deck above. Tom slipped behind a barrel in a shadowy corner of the hold. Not long afterwards, as dawn was breaking, Luggole Spain came heavily down the stairs.

"Sleep tight, Tregorey?" he sneered. "In need of a drink, are ye?"

"No," I lied. In truth, my mouth was as dry as ashes and I was desperate for water.

"Well, ye soon will be. Gets mighty hot down 'ere. An' t'make sure no meddlin' constable takes it into 'is 'ead to come lookin' for ye, we'll be 'eading out to sea while ye makes up yer's mind. We'll return, o'course – when ye's ready to tell us where them jewels lie."

He stomped over to the stairway and paused, one foot on the bottom step. "An' if ye takes too long to offer us your help, Tregorey, I might arrange for ye to have a drink o' sea water. Ye'll 'ave got quite a bellyful when we're finished with 'e! Ha! Ha!"

With that, he clambered back to the deck where we heard him waking Jago, Cadan, Kitto and Ruan. The sound of the anchor being raised soon followed and within the half hour the schooner was rising and falling with the swell of the open sea.

Whatever noble plans of rescue Tom might have had, he was now just as much a prisoner aboard the pirate vessel as Oloudah and I were. To be honest, I felt like crying. Judging by the tone of his voice, I believe Tom felt the same.

Oloudah was made of tougher stuff. "When you've been captured and shipped across the sea as a slave, you learn to be strong," he said quietly. "And you also learn to never, ever give up."

My friend's wise and brave words shook me out of my misery. There must be a way out, I thought. There must be.... I looked around. To my left was a gun port, not far above the waterline. Yes, it might just be possible....

"Listen," I whispered. "I've got an idea. It's dangerous and probably won't work, but it's the best I can think of."

I explained my plan to the others, who reckoned it was worth a try. The trouble was, the trickiest bits of it depended on me.

Chapter 10

Treasure

When we were ready, Tom went back into hiding and Oloudah started groaning loudly. The noise brought Luggole lurching down the steps once more. I said Oloudah was sick and needed a doctor. The pirate laughed and said he'd rather have King George himself on board than a "swindling sawbones".

"But Oloudah's my friend," I stammered huskily. "You must do something!"

"It's ye as must do summat," retorted Luggole with a hideous grin.

And so it was, slowly and with a great show of reluctance, that I agreed to do what Luggole wanted. If they sailed back to the bay off Port-au-Prince, I sighed, I'd show them where the chest containing the McKinley jewels had fallen into the sea.

"An seein' as we don't swim," said Luggole, "it's ye as'll 'ave to fish it out for us. Then ye and yer slave'll be set free, and 'e can see as many sawbones as 'e pleases."

The brigand was clearly relieved that I'd accepted his terms. He became all chuckles and smiles, and called me his "young friend". He even got Jago to bring us bread and water.

The crew swung the schooner swung round and we headed back towards

Hispaniola. When we were within sight of the shore, Luggole undid the padlock and opened the shackles around my ankles. He then closed the padlock. I watched carefully, as he slid the key into the left hand pocket of his coat.

Cadan lowered the anchor over the reef to the north of Port-au-Prince. Jago escorted me onto the swaying deck and placed me close beside the captain. I stared at the sea, trying to recall exactly where the chest had disappeared. A few yards to my right I noticed an area of darker water. Suddenly, the picture was as clear in my mind as on the day it happened. Yes, that was the spot alright....

"There!" I cried, pointing towards the dark patch. "I think that's where the jewel chest fell!"

With the attention of Luggole and the others focussed on where I was indicating, I pretended to lose my balance and fell heavily against the captain's side. His left side.

As my fingers closed about the key and I drew it out of the pirate's pocket unnoticed, a wave of relief surged through me. I'd completed the first – and probably most difficult – step of my plan.

Now for step two. I took off my shirt ready for the swim and hid the key in the waistband of my breeches. I'd begin with a general search of the area, I explained to Luggole. Once I had located the chest, I'd return to the ship for a rope with which to heave it aboard. The captain and his men would only have to pull – and the jewels would be theirs.

"An' ye and yer slave friend'll be as free as birds!" cackled Luggole, grinning round at his companions. "Sea birds!"

I shuddered to think what would happen if things went wrong. Being buried alive at sea was not my idea of a happy ending.

I plunged into the warm water and dived down under the boat, pretending to be searching for the chest. On the far side of the hull I swam up the gun port. To my relief, it swung open and Tom's hand grabbed the key.

Step two, I thought. So far, so good. I swam back under the hull. "Nothing here!" I called to the men on the deck. I indicated the darker water I'd pointed out earlier. "I'll go and look over there."

I made my way with slow, easy strokes then floated for a while to get my breath back. I was playing for time. When I was ready, I filled my lungs, kicked my legs in the air and dived beneath the waves. I was in a different world, a silent blue-green land of brilliant, timid fish and seaweed like a mermaid's hair waving gently back and forth in the current.

The chest, already crusted with barnacles, was exactly where I hoped it would be. It lay on its side, unopened, in about 20 feet of water. I'd have no trouble swimming down to that depth.

Step three of my plan should have come into operation by now, and as

I headed for the ship I expected to see Tom and Oloudah waving at me. Instead, I was greeted by the grinning faces of the five pirates.

I started to panic. What had gone wrong? Had the key broken in the padlock? Had my friends made their move and been overpowered? When the pirates gave no sign of having been disturbed, I forced myself to concentrate on the business in hand. Patience, I told myself. Patience.

Ruan threw me the end of a rope and, towing it behind me, I swam slowly back to the reef. I dived down to the chest without difficulty, knotted the line round a stout brass handle on the side and burst back to the surface.

Still no sign of my friends. I was getting desperate.

"Haul away!" I yelled. Unfortunately, raising the chest was easier than I had imagined – rather like drawing in a large fish on a line. Only once did I have to dive down and free it when it became wedged between a couple of rocks.

Sooner than I had wanted, the chest lay dripping at Luggole's feet. I followed up a rope ladder. Oloudah and Tom were nowhere to be seen. A terrible thought ran through my mind. They couldn't have abandoned me, could they, escaping through the gun port and swimming for the shore?

Cadan and Jago grabbed me the moment my feet touched the deck.

"Oi!" I cried. "You said you'd let me go free!"

"Changed me mind, m'dear," snarled Luggole. "It's not just treasure as I'm after. It's revenge!"

The two pirates held me tight as the captain kicked at the rusted lock on the side of the chest. It soon broke, and with a cry of delight Luggole threw back the lid.

It was an extraordinary sight. Priceless gold, silver and jewels lay like glittering eggs in the nest of some magical bird. But I had no eyes for the treasure. My gaze was fixed only on the chest that held it.

Luggole dipped in his hand and lifted out a string of pearls. "Bootiful!" he crowed, looking up at me. "An' when we've tipped them all out, this 'ere box'll make a snug little coffin for ye, Tregorey. 'Bout right size, d'ye reckon?"

"Please!" I begged, glancing desperately around for some sign of Tom and Oloudah, then turning to Ruan. "I did rescue ye from the sea once, remember?"

"That be true," muttered Ruan. "Maybe we could do summat else but drown 'im in that there casket?"

"Silence, dog!" roared Luggole. "If I say 'e drowns, 'e drowns!"

I could see no escape. My foolish decision to travel alone to the Caribbean had ended in a terrible disaster.

"Oh my poor father!" I cried. "For his sake have mercy, Mr Spain. I beg you!"

"Mercy?" he echoed, holding up a gleaming emerald to the sunlight. "No, not mercy, Tregorey. Like I said, it's revenge I'm after. Revenge!"

"And revenge is what you will not have!" cried a familiar voice. Scarcely able to believe my ears, I glanced up to see Oloudah and Tom emerging from the door to the stern cabin. Each sported a pair of pistols they'd found there. I almost fainted with relief.

Luggole uttered a vile curse and sprang towards them. A shot rang out and he fell to the deck, clutching his left thigh. "Just grazed him," said Oloudah. "But I don't think he'll be giving us any more trouble."

And he didn't. Nor did any of the others after we had locked them in the cabin alongside their wounded leader. Our first thought was to hand them over to the port authorities. As they would probably all be hanged for sure, we changed our minds. For the sake of Ruan, who seemed a half-decent fellow, we entrusted them to the mercy of the sea.

We threw the schooner's sails over the side and broke her wheel. Then, having cut her anchor rope, we released the prisoners. Covering them with the pistols, we packed up the treasure chest and clambered into the skiff that had brought me to the vessel. A stiff offshore breeze was now blowing and it carried the drifting schooner swiftly out into the Atlantic Ocean. Before long, she and her dastardly crew were no more than a distant speck on the horizon.

As I rowed towards the shore, Tom explained how he had made it to shore in the *Neptune's* leaky lifeboat, then tracked me down. All Jamaica, he said, had buzzed with story of an escaped slave, a pair of pirates who had stolen a schooner, and a young lad who had hired a fishing boat to take him to Hispaniola. Putting two and two together, he had worked out what was going on and made his way to Port-au-Prince. The rest, he grinned, I already knew.

"And how come ye took so long getting out of the hold after I'd given you the key?" I asked.

"Sorry!" laughed Tom. "We couldn't come rushing up the ladder and expect to overcome five heavily-armed pirates, could we? We had to find weapons first, then sneak through the ship so we'd come up behind them."

Once ashore, we opened the chest and stared again at the breath-taking array of diamonds, rubies, emeralds and pearls. Though the seawater had tarnished their gold and silver settings, the jewels themselves shone as bright as they had ever done. No wonder Luggole had wanted to get his hands on them! They were worth a king's ransom.

* * *

Their value was confirmed by their rightful owner, Jacob McKinley, who we eventually tracked down in London. He had given up all hope long ago of ever seeing his inheritance. So pleased was he at finding it intact, and so amazed was he by our honesty in returning it to him, he generously handed over half of it to be split between the three of us.

Tom used his fortune to set up a seafaring school for boys. Oloudah returned to his family in Africa where, I last heard, he was organizing successful resistance to the evil slave trade.

And me? The first thing I did with my money was send another ten guineas to old Joseph in Jamaica, in case my original deposit had not covered the cost of a new boat. The rest I gave to my long-suffering father. He and I still live together in the Friendly Frenchman. And I still pour the ale on windy nights and listen to Old Jacob Winstanley singing his dismal sea shanties. But these days it's different. When he sings of the bottom of the sea, a strange feeling comes over me.

You see, unlike everyone else joining in that mournful song, I've actually been there.

THE END

FICTI●N EXPRESS

THE READERS TAKE CONTROL!

Have you ever wanted to change the course of a plot, change a character's destiny, tell an author what to write next?

Well, now you can!

'The Pirate's Revenge' was originally written for the award-winning interactive e-book website Fiction Express.

Fiction Express e-books are published in gripping weekly episodes. At the end of each episode, readers are given voting options to decide where the plot goes next. They vote online and the winning vote is then conveyed to the author who writes the next episode, in real time, according to the readers' most popular choice.

www.fictionexpress.co.uk

WINNER
Education Resources
Award for Innovation

FICTION EXPRESS

TALK TO THE AUTHORS

The Fiction Express website features a blog where readers can interact with the authors while they are writing. An exciting and unique opportunity!

FANTASTIC TEACHER RESOURCES

Each weekly Fiction Express episode comes with a PDF of teacher resources packed with ideas to extend the text.

"The teaching resources are fab and easily fill a whole week of literacy lessons!"
Rachel Humphries, teacher at Westacre Middle School

The Pirate's Secret
by Stewart Ross

One windswept winter's evening, Arden Tregory listens enthralled as his father tells him of his 'golden secret' and how he once outwitted the notorious one-eared pirate Lambert 'Luggole' Spain. The very next day his father is kidnapped and disappears, so Arden decides to set off to the Caribbean in search of him.

But how will he travel the 5000 miles of dangerous Atlantic Ocean, and will he succeed in finding his only living relative?

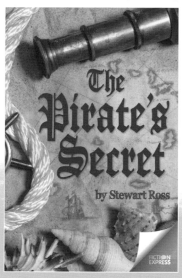

ISBN 978-1-78322-552-1

FICTI●N EXPRESS

Threads
by Sharon Gosling

Young Charlie Thwaite works in Stanton's mill and is best friends with the mill-owner's daughter, Clara. When Charlie's father is wrongly accused of sabotaging Stanton's new spinning machines, it's up to Charlie and Clara to prove his innocence.

Will they discover the real culprit in time to save both Charlie's father and the mill?

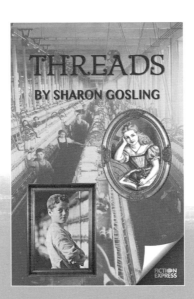

ISBN 978-1-78322-557-6

FICTI🗩N EXPRESS

Rémy Brunel and the Circus Horse
by Sharon Gosling

"Roll up, roll up, and see the greatest show on Earth!" Rémy Brunel loves her life in the circus – riding elephants, practising tightrope tricks and dazzling audiences. But when two new magicians arrive at the circus, everyone is wary of them. What exactly are they up to? What secrets are they trying to hide? Should Rémy and her new friend Matthias trust them?

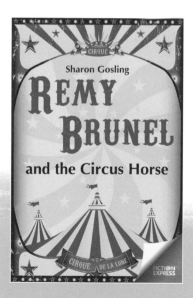

ISBN 978-1-78322-469-2

FICTI✏N EXPRESS

The Time Detectives:
The Mystery of Maddie Musgrove
by Alex Woolf

When Joe Smallwood goes to stay with his Uncle Theo and cousin Maya life seems dull, until he finds a strange smartphone nestling beside a gravestone. The phone enables Joe and Maya to become time-travelling detectives and takes them on an exciting adventure back to Victorian times. Can they prove maidservant Maddie Musgrove's innocence? Can they save her from the gallows?

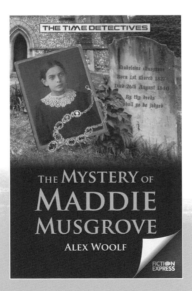

ISBN 978-1-78322-459-3

The Time Detectives:
The Disappearance of Danny Doyle
by Alex Woolf

When the Time Detectives, Joe and Maya, stumble upon an old house in the middle of a wood, its occupant has a sad tale to tell. Michael was evacuated to Dorset during World War II with his twin brother, Danny. While there, Danny mysteriously disappeared and was never heard from again. Can Joe and Maya succeed where the police failed, journey back to 1941 and trace Michael's missing brother?

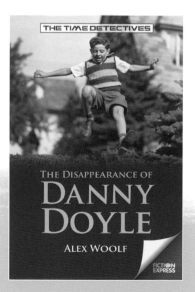

THE TIME DETECTIVES

THE DISAPPEARANCE OF
DANNY
DOYLE
ALEX WOOLF

FICTION EXPRESS

ISBN 978-1-78322-458-6

About the Author

Prizewinning author Stewart Ross taught at all levels in Britain, the USA, the Middle East and Sri Lanka before becoming a full-time writer twenty-six years ago. Some 280 (lost count) of his books have been published, including two novels for adults and 35 works of fiction for children. He has written plays, lyrics and poetry, too. His books have been translated into around 20 languages.

When not writing, Stewart enjoys travel, music, sport, theatre and ambling through the woods near his home. As a change from the large garden hut in which he works, Stewart ventures forth to schools, colleges and universities in Britain, France and elsewhere to talk about writing and pass on his passion for words.